Eat Up
Little Donkey

By Rindert Kromhout & Annemarie van Haeringen

GECKO PRESS

"Lunchtime, Little Donkey!"
says Mama.
"Guess what I've made for you."

"Open wide."

"Won't,"
says Little Donkey.

"Here comes a train!"
says Mama.

"My tummy says no."

"Here comes a plane!"
says Little Donkey.

"Oh no, you don't,"
says Mama.

"Watch me fly!"
laughs Little Donkey.

"Come on, rascal,"
says Mama.
"We're off to the park."

"Hello, ducks.

Little Donkey isn't hungry.

Eat as much as you like."

"But Mama, I do want it!"

One bite for the ducks...

and one for Little Donkey.